Newsman Telling

Whoppers

by

Bo Noir

Gueraville Books

ISBN: 978-0-9904848-7-5

Editing by Natasha Nouveau

Cover Illustration by Sophia Michailidou

For the good men with bad plights they will
never be able to fight.

- Bo

Chapter 1

Hank Pendleton was the top newsman on network television. Ten years at the top of the ratings. He was ten Emmy Awards and two Peabody Awards above the competition. He got ten million viewers each night. And he had ten inches of truth in his Armani trousers.

If there was breaking news anywhere in the world, Hank was there. If there was a single lady witness to that breaking news, Hank was there too. If there was a bi-curious roommate of that witness, Hank was headed right over in a sec. And if there was a divorced mother of that bi-curious roommate, Hank brought them together and delivered scoops, hard facts and broke their stories open wide.

Yes, Hank "Motherfucking" Pendleton was the luckiest S.O.B. on the goddamned face of the earth. Not only did he have a choice multi-million dollar bachelor pad in the heart of Manhattan, he only had to work half an hour a day! Of course, there was preparation for his nightly news broadcast. There were stories to file and facts to check. Lucky for Hank, there were underlings and minions to do all of that. He had the most brilliant team of interns in journalism. All were handpicked by Hank from a pile of resumes that included photographs and sizzle reels.

He would walk up to the news station 60 minutes before his broadcast. Thirty of those minutes were for his special news meeting, where he planned the show with his producer. Yet most days, his producer would ready the show with the staff in the conference room while Hank got a personal update from his private intern, Jessie Diamond. Jessie had been one of over a thousand applicants for the exclusive Pendleton internship. Her lube-scented resume and accompanying Polaroid got her the gig, and she was great at her job.

Jessie stands in the doorway to Hank's office. She is wearing a short, flirty, ruffled skirt—way too girly for this workplace, but it isn't his job to tell her that—and a pale pink, almost sheer blouse. He eyes her up and down, paying particular attention to her long, lean, perfectly self-tanned legs, the crux of her thighs, her tiny, touchable waist, and her plump but pleasingly proportioned boobies. If he weren't sure of her age, 20½, he would have thought she'd gotten lost on a high school field trip.

She steps into his office, the clack of her high heels startling him away from the dirty thoughts bouncing around in his mind. He cocks his head at her and raises an eyebrow.

"Can I help you with something, Jessie?"

"I was going to ask you the same thing," she demurs. Honest to God, she ducks her head, her cheeks pink, her shoulders sag, and she peeks up at him under her fluttering lashes. Her blue eyes sparkle. His eyes and his boner can't look away.

She beams. A full mouth of

perfect, straight, and bright white teeth greets him.

"Hank, no one has anything for me to do and I am very bored. I was hoping you...", she hesitates and he leans forward, encouraging her to continue, "...would be able to help me out."

"Well..." he scratches his chin as he tilts his head to study the ceiling, acting the part of a serious thinker. Already, he knows what she can do for him.

"Yes?" She is clinging to his promise of an answer. "I will do anything."

He lowers his head to stare at her. Did he really hear that? Did she emphasize that 'any' a bit too much? As in 'I will do ANYthing?' He searches her face for a sign that what he thought he heard was exactly what she wanted him to hear.

She stares right back. Her eyes are guileless and innocent. Considering the way she is dressed, he's positive it is all part of a little game she is playing. She has sex kitten written all over her, she always has.

"ANYthing?" he asks, more than sure now. She nods. Her tongue slips from between her bright pink lips and she licks across them. His cock grows and thickens in his slacks at that gesture and he hopes to hell she isn't a tease. Teasing is fine. Being a tease is not.

"Yes," she purrs.

"Well, I am a little stiff and

would love a massage. How are you with your hands?"

She lifts her arms, shaking out her hands. Clasping them together, she sets about stretching each digit and rubbing her palms briskly to warm them. He watches her. She shrugs and loosens her shoulders, looking from him to the office door. He reads her mind and crosses the room to shut the door. And locks it.

"Show me where, Hank."

He grins as he returns to her side. With all the casualness of a man certain to get what he wants from an incredibly young, beautiful, and eager intern, he unbuckles his trousers. He snaps off his suspenders and pushes the dark linen pants down his legs. He eases his black satin boxers down as well.

"Here. Very stiff here." He looks down at his thick, throbbing, fully erect cock. It is standing tall, tight against his stomach. He grabs the base, and wrapping his fist around his steely length, he pumps himself. A groan rips from his throat. His eyes close in pleasure. He continues pumping up and down his shaft until he feels her warm palms cover his fist. He slows, glancing down.

She's on her knees, mouth open, eyes alive. He lets go, allowing her to take over. And take over she does. She wraps her own fist around his base and lowers his cock until she can press sloppy kisses to his cockhead. She slurps all around his cock, coating it in her saliva. His eyes never wander from her, entranced as he is with her worship of him.

Her other hand—the one not holding his cock—slips underneath and lifts his balls. She massages the testicular organs, ever so often pressing her fingertips along the seam from his ass to his balls. No one has ever done that before and he can't believe what he's missed out on. It feels incredible.

The sweet intern eases his cock inside her mouth and he almost wishes she would stop teasing him so. He is so close to coming already. He can't fuck her mouth, as he really wants. She sucks him deep and relaxes her throat to allow him to fill her completely. He may not be able to fully fuck her face, but he can enjoy a little fun.

Digging trimmed nails into

her scalp, he holds her still and thrusts three times. As he pulls out, a trail of saliva connects them both. He's still, memorizing the scene—loving every second.

She looks ready for more. He reaches down to cup her chin and lifts her to her feet.

"Get up on the desk, Jessie, and spread your legs."
She does, right after she pushes her panties down and kicks them at him. He lets the slip of lace bounce off his suit dress shirt and laughs. He steps into her spread legs and hauls her ass to the edge of the large metal desk.
"Put your legs on my shoulders."

This, too, she does. She is quiet, sexy, incredibly flexible, and already very wet. She takes direction well and obviously loves a good fucking. All this he notices as he holds his cock steady and plunges forward. He slips inside her sheath and begins pounding away. She moans and whimpers. She begs him for more: rougher, harder, faster sex. His name is a constant plea on her lips. She works her blouse open and cups her own breasts, playing with them as he takes his pleasure from her.

He wants her completely, needs to hold on and make this last. But he can't. She's too much. Too perfect. Her juice forms a puddle on his desk, the scent of her arousal filling the room. His balls slap her ass as he quickens his pace. When he comes, he erupts with a huge load—pulling out just in time to wet her thighs.

Stepping back, he lowers her

legs. She dangles them against the side of his desk. Reaching down, she gathers some of his spunk on a forefinger. She sucks her digit clean, maintaining eye contact with Hank throughout. He forgets how to think.

"Anything else, Hank?"

"Uuuuuhhh. Wow." He stutters and grunts like a drunken ape as she puts on her clothes and waltzes out of his office like a dream. Damn, did that just happen, he thinks. Yes, in Hank Pendleton's world, it happens quite a lot.

After a tryst, he would take another 30 minutes for wardrobe and makeup with his makeup artist, who on some days was more of a make-out artist. She was, of course, handpicked from the makeup artist resume pile that included pictures and sizzle reels. Then Hank would settle into his anchor's chair. He would look straight into the living rooms of America and read from a teleprompter for 22 minutes. The other 8 minutes in his broadcast were made up of commercial breaks. Lucky for Hank, the network allowed him to bring a computer tablet to his news desk, and outfitted the studio with Wi-Fi. This way, Hank could browse new sites such as BigBreastworldwide.com and Camgirlslive.xxx for up-to-the-minute reports.

After signing off with his usual, "Thank you for watching and good night and sleep tight America!", he would meet with his producer, Barry Dreck, for a rundown of the broadcast.

"Hank, we have some up-to-the-minute ratings reports here. I thought you would like to know right away."

"Boy, Barry, you know me well. How did we do?" Hank asked.

"Pretty fucking fabulous. You are number one with women—"

"Shit, Barry, I could have told you that!"

"Ahahahahahahahahahahahah ahahahahahahahahahaha! You're amazing! Ahahahahahahahahahahahahahaha hahahahahahaha!" Barry said.

"What else?" Hank asked.

"You are the most trusted

anchor on college campuses, too. Now that reminds me, this might be a good time for you to do a book tour. Get out there, feel out the young people!"

"Barry, if they need to be felt, then feel them I must!" said Hank, as he held out his hands in a groping fashion.

"Ahahahahahahahahahahahah ahahahahahahahahahaha! Whoa, my back! It hurts to laugh so much. Ahahahahaha! You're killing me, Hank. Ahahahahahahahaha!" Barry said.

"OK. I'm bored. Let's talk about this later, Barry. I got to go. I got a hot date tonight!"

Hank Pendleton didn't date lightly. He had a date with the hottest R&B singer in the world,

Beyionna. She usually dated rappers and hip hop moguls, but ever since a new media conglomerate bought her record label, she had been encouraged to reach out across platforms. She was to make connections and achieve synergy and all that corporate bullshit.

Hank stepped out of his anchorman suit and stepped into his date suit. The only difference between the two was that the date suit was pre-musked for arousing a lady's olfactory senses. And Hank liked to dab a little musk on his sweet spot too, in case things got cozy before the dessert was served.

Stepping out of his stretch limousine, Hank waltzed up to Chez Fartesse, the best French restaurant in New York. In the middle, at the most visible table, was Beyionna. Uncommonly on time, she was sipping a lemon drop martini and dabbing her cleavage with it. She wore a stunning Versace gown that didn't leave anything to the imagination. Hank stepped up to the table and presented his shaking hand to the beautiful lady.

"Hello, I'm Hank Pendleton, America's number one newsman. You must be Beyionna?"

"Yeah, that's me. Damn, you're tall for a white man! I dated ballers before, but damn, you as tall as them!"

"6 foot 7 and worth the climb! Hahahaahahahahahahaahahahahahaha hahahaahahahahahahaha!"

Beyionna scrunched her face

as Hank laughed at his own joke for a solid two minutes. It didn't bother her. The label was paying her for the evening by the hour and it would get her points on sales of her new concert video. So she could put up with anything tonight, even if that included being interviewed and hit on by Hank Pendleton.

Hank didn't date in any normal fashion. He always talked to people like he was interviewing them for his news program. Tonight wasn't any different. As soon as they sat down, he got into it.

"So tell me, Beyionna, at this point in your career, 15 million albums sold, 12 Grammy awards, a fashion line, a makeup line, a bestselling memoir, what do you think is your next challenge?"

Hank asked.

Beyionna didn't date lightly either. She was a consummate professional. She could turn any question asked by anyone into a question about her and what she was doing. Taking another sip of her lemon drop, she retorted smoothly.

"Hank, it's funny that you ask. Is it OK if I call you Hank? Well, anyway, you know, I'm just an artist trying to keep it real, you know. What gets me out of bed are my fans. What keeps me grounded is my family. Really I'm ready to break more barriers and stay at the forefront, you know what I'm saying? Artistry and fashion are both part of building the Beyionna brand. At the same time I'm keeping my ear to the streets, you know?"

"So you want to act?" asked Hank.

"You're damn right. Sitcom actors can make a million per episode, movie actors 10 million. Shit, that's the business I want to be in. You know any directors, Hank?"

Hank knew directors; they just made films available exclusively on the Internet and in certain pants-optional movie theaters in rough parts of the city. But he did know one producer who could help Beyionna out. He gave her his number and remarked that the most important thing for him was helping young people live their dreams.

"Aw, you're sweet," Beyionna said.

They continued to banter about the media industry, and after the dessert was served they shared a cab to his place. Hank Pendleton was a get-it-done kind of guy. Courting megastars was his middle name. His bachelor pad was fully equipped for actresses, models, singers, cheerleaders, hairdressers, makeup artists, interns, and the occasional head of state to feel at ease and want to slip into something more comfortable.

He lived in a triplex loft on the Upper East Side. The elevator went straight to his door, and he'd had his butler lay out some Champagne and strawberries for the evening.

"You know, Beyionna, in all my years covering wars, I don't think I've seen a goddess worth dying for until tonight. You are as bangin' as you wanna be!"

Beyionna, since she really didn't date lightly, decided to negotiate a bit before the expected sexual tryst.

"You know, Hank, a two-part report on my upcoming world tour would certainly put me in a dress-dropping mood," she said.

"Honey, how about three parts on the network and an Internet-only behind-the-scenes special?"

"Wow, you really are the best newsman in town. You got yourself a scoop. Now, why don't you drop them pants?"

Hank obliged. Shimmy shimmy, one flick of his belt and his trousers hit the floor. He wore his trousers loose for this reason:

speed. His boxer shorts were silk with a peek-a-boo window in the middle for easy access.

He stripped off his jacket and white shirt, but left his tie and wife beater on. He also kept on his shoes for extra traction. Beyionna did her part by dropping that dress and revealing her treasures that Hank had searched for on gossip sites.

"Dark, perky, uniformly round. My dear, your nipples are chocolate gold medals in the sport of being Fiiiiiine!"

"You're not so bad yourself."

Hank loved it when women complimented him. He stepped up to her nude body and grabbed her with his manly arms. She fit perfectly against him. He felt good against her, and she found out that those ten-inch rumors were true.

Beyionna reached down, grabbed his straight cock in her hand, and started stroking it. Back and forth, her hands glided ever so tightly. When the friction got too rough, she would lube her grip with a little bit of spit. He really loved it when her palm caressed his little newsman. He used this time to roam her booty, looking for the perfect squeezing spot. Her round and ample behind felt good to knead, like two massive mounds of dough. He nibbled at her neck and took in all of her exotic scents.

Beyionna smelled great. She wore her own brand of perfume, "Whilin", and it smelled like candy from a caramel store. Looking deep into each other's eyes, they kissed. Beyionna used her free hand to stroke the back of

Hank's neck. Their bodies melded together and they became one unit that moved to the rhythm of their passions.

Hank wanted to know what it was like to fuck a 12-time Grammy Award winner. He didn't need to get her on the bed to do it. He swung her across his bar, picking her booty up and plopping it down. Her pussy was at the height of his chest, but he fixed that by lowering his mouth to meet it. Ah, more Whilin scent, he thought. She was courteous enough to spray it everywhere.

Using his tongue, he freestyled a rap love song into her body at a dance remix pace. She wrapped her legs around his head. She was not going to let go until she came.

"Yeah, lick that pussy, fool! Tell it, baby, tell it like it is!" she purred.

His breath sped up and so did his tongue. He was relishing every moment as he ate her out on his Italian marble counter. Every now and then, his head would pop up to brag about the place.

"That counter your ass is sitting on is Italian marble from the region of Carrara. Notice it keep keeps your ass quite cool despite—Gulp!"

Beyionna just pushed his head back down to her pussy when his bragging dragged on too long. She was out to get her nut that night. And as she got closer to it, she started to let him know.

"Faster, baby. Faster, baby.

Ooo!"

"As you approach your orgasm, tell the viewers what is going through your mind as— Gulp?" Hank whispered.

"Fuck you talking about? What viewers? Eat that pussy, you ain't signing off yet!" she yelled.

Her nimble body bucked back and forth as she kicked her heels over him. She loved this. And when she finally got there, tasting that sweet feeling of coming, she grabbed a tuft of Hank's hair and messed it all up. Then she slapped him hard on the side of his face, all while holding him down and pressing his lips hard against her.

"Aaaaaaah! Yes! Yes! You got it! You got it, oooooooooooooh!"

Beyionna reached her climax and promptly pushed Hank's head away from her as she exploded on the inside. He fell backwards, hitting his naked ass on the floor.

"Ow! That's a Granville slate kitchen floor. Dang that smarts!"

"Smart is right, you smart motherfucker! You got me off quick. Shit, I still have time to make Zay-J's party!" she exclaimed.

A curious look fell over Hank's face. He looked down at his erect boner and wondered how this could be happening. No woman had ever left him in the lurch like that.

"You're leaving?!? To go to Zay-J's party?!? Holy smokes, I just realized I wasn't invited. But,

but, what about this?!?" he yelled, as he pointed to his crotch.

"Jerk off to my sex tape, I know you have it!"

Hank nodded in affirmation. He did indeed have her sex tape, in HD no less. While it wouldn't be as great as the real thing, Hank couldn't really complain. Beyionna was a superstar; she placed much higher in the entertainment industry pecking order than a nightly newsman. No wonder he'd done all of the licking and she was doing all the leaving.

"Beyionna, you're leaving me so unsatisfied. Was there a point in your illustrious coming fit that you considered playing a more sustained role in this evening's shagging?"

"Hank, from an artist's perspective, I like to lay down my vocals only when I'm really feeling the beat, you know what I'm saying. But that doesn't mean we can't remix it down the road."

"Well said, and congratulations on your perfume line. I inhaled loads of it when my nose was nostril deep in your snatch, and let me tell you, it's gonna make those millennials go crazy!"

"They are 64% of my intended demographic. Later, Hank Pendleton. See you on the flip side!"

"And goodnight Beyionna! Thank you for coming and good night and sleep tight America!" he said with a wave as she walked out the door.

He held his waving hand up for a full 30 seconds after she had left, just like he did when he signed off the air.

Yes, Hank Pendleton, top newsman, was completely fucking insane.

Chapter 2

There was a time when the most trusted person in America was the television newsman. He was the true teller of the truth. If he said it, it happened; no exceptions. But America has become a much more cynical place. Nobody trusts the media, and with good reason. The cable networks are a cesspool of lies and bias. The Internet, is all bullshit. The only place where there is still a smidgen of integrity is the nightly news on the major networks.

The other two major networks lagged behind Hank's channel in the ratings. They had veteran journalists with impeccable reputations. But Hank; he had a problem. Well, Hank had many problems. Hank had a million problems. But the worst and most pertinent to his job was his casual attitude towards the truth. If he felt he could make a story more exciting, he tended to embellish the facts a little bit. Sometimes he embellished the facts a lot. Sometimes he just plain made shit up. Some thought of Hank as too big to fail. He brought in the dough for the network and was well-liked in the newsroom. But others questioned his integrity and thought he was a ticking time bomb that could destroy the whole news organization.

One prime example of his special brand of crazy revolved around a trip to Iraq during the first years of the war. He was in a convoy of three helicopters that was bringing supplies to troops. The first helicopter had no journalists in it. The second had no journalists. The third had no good journalists, but Hank was there along with his producer. They received word that the first helicopter had been struck by a surface-to-air missile. The missile didn't detonate; it only cut through the fuselage. The struck helicopter was about 30 minutes of flight time ahead of Hank's helicopter.

After the attack, all three helicopters were told to land and wait until a massive dust storm passed. Hank was in the back of the third helicopter, strapped to a chair. He had taken a Quaalude, a couple of sleeping pills, three melatonin gummies and a double shot of whiskey as soon as he heard that the first chopper was hit. Hank was a lover, not a fighter. And he was wearing his new pants. He felt that if he was out cold, he wouldn't be scared and wouldn't shit his pants if things got nasty. He hoped the soldiers would protect him.

His minders, fixers and protectors were Pvts. Darryl Mixon and Lori Lee. They were given the task of babysitting the big baby anchorman and make making sure he didn't get killed. They were quite fond of him. He made sure to slip them quite a lot of cash to break protocol and escort him off base to indulge in his various vices. They provided his drugs, women and confidence while he goofed off and didn't do his job. The rest of the crew respected Hank's wishes and were happy that he just stayed out of the way. So they let him sleep, while the helicopters were grounded for 30 hours. Hank slept for 29½ of those hours and woke up at the end, just before takeoff.

"What the fuck just happened?"

Barry, his brownnosing producer, filled him in on what was going on.

"Hank, so that one over there got shot at. Now we've been here chilling until this dust storm passes and we're about to take off. Another 10 hours to base, then we'll file this report."

"Alright, whatever. Wake me when we're there!" Hank said.

He put on his noise-cancelling headphones, popped a white mystery pill Lori Lee gave him and went back to sleep. It was amazing how he could hibernate, then stay up for 40 hours at a time when he was partying.

When they arrived back at the base where the news headquarters was, he entered the studio and delivered 100% pure Hank Pendleton magic.

"Hello, I'm Hank Pendleton, reporting from Iraq. We got a glimpse of true battle, and boy, are we lucky to be alive. We were on a mission of mercy, full of risks. We were be flying over hostile territory, and that's when things got ugly. One of the helicopters in our group was shot at and hit. Fire was coming at us. We dropped and took cover in a dust storm until it was safe to take off again."

From there he continued to pontificate and make it look like he was right in the action. Then, five months later, he went on his network's own late night variety show and said this:

"So here we are in Iraq, flying over enemy territory, knowing they were going to be firing at us on the way. I could smell the sulfurous, explosive spice of hatred-filled missiles as they whizzed past my head. My helicopter was hit and we held on for dear life and quickly descended to avoid more fire and a huge dust storm that threatened to swallow us whole like a giant red whale made of earth and sand."

One year later at a presentation at a prestigious journalist journalism college, he said this:

"So I'm at the flight controls of this 500-million-dollar helicopter. I have bombs and bullets at the ready, fighting for

freedom in the Cradle of Terror.
I'm trying to protect and give
cover to the helicopter in front of
us. It is smoking from the rocket-
propelled grenades. As I look
Death in the face, another missile
comes straight at us. Luckily it
doesn't detonate but it hits us and
ricochets off the airframe, nearly
taking off the head of my
producer, Barry. The pilot of the
other chopper tells me to turn
around, save our skins and retreat.
But no, that's not the Pendleton
Way! I took the 50 caliber and I
started mowing the lawn with
bullets. Ping! Pow! Ping! Dropped
a couple of biggity bombs on their
candy asses and lit up my Havana
cigar when it was over!"

Three years later at the bar in
in the Plaza hotel, to the lonely
wife of a European diplomat, he
said this:

"So I heard this voice. I heard a question in the air. 'Can you be a world-class journalist and a brave hero at the same time?' And I said, 'Yes, God, I can.' And as our chopper was taking fire, bullets whizzing past my face, I was blinded by acrid smoke from my own burning jumpsuit. I could have thrown in the towel. Cashed my hero's ticket in for a deckchair and cool drink beyond St. Peter's Gates. But I used this technique I learned from SEAL Team 6: I closed my eyes and let the "Force" guide my hands. I shot down four enemy planes and miraculously was able to shoot through the chain that was keeping this little brown puppy from running out of a burning yard in the distance. We landed just three feet shy of a 1,000-foot-high cliff. And the first thing that popped into my head was, damn, if I make it home alive, the first thing I'm going to do is devote my life to helping young urban teens live their dreams. The second thing I'm going to do is buy you a drink, at this bar, at this very moment, because you are what we are fighting for, my dear."

Three years later in the office of the head of the news division of his network, Wes Evans, a gray-haired corporate suit said this:

"Hey, Hank, thanks for coming in. Well, I don't really know how to say this, but, well, it has to be said. There is a web-based news service called Fuzzbeed News, and they, um, have been keeping some tabs on you."

"Tabs?" said Hank. His brow was starting to sweat. He knew the full extent of all the things that could be considered 'tabs' on him. And most of them were bad.

"Yes, tabs. You see, you've been on the air for a long time. You've been on this program, and a lot of other news programs, and even some non-news programs. We think it's great. Going on a comedy show makes you more relatable. Cross branding. Synergy. All that good shit. But, um, you know how you have that habit of stretching the truth a bit?"

"No. What do you mean?"

"Um, you know what I mean, and you're bullshitting me now. See, this website has been keeping tabs on you and they have, like, a running tally of all the, um, exaggerations you have made over the years. They have it story by story, in a tidy organization of rows and columns. The layperson can see how you have changed your stories over time. Plus, they have audio and video of you saying all of these things."

"Oh. Well, is that going to be a problem?"

"Problem? Fuck, man, problem?!? Yes, asshole, it's going to be a problem when the American public expects you to be on-the-mark honest with them all the time. Your credibility is the only thing that gives you power as a newsman. Without it, you're just another blogger, un-fact-checked and unimportant. And since you are the face of the network, your credibility is the network's credibility. And our news division's credibility brings us 500 million fucking dollars a year. And when this Fuzzbeed thing goes wide, maybe some of that ca-ching, ca-ching might go from being a river of dollars to a trickle. You catch my drift?" Wes said.

"Umm," Hank hummed. He was speechless. Part of him was terrified he might lose his job. Part of him was relieved that this had nothing to do with his activities on that trip to Cambodia a few years ago. He'd gone to the dark side on that trip. How dark? Life in prison dark. So he listened to Wes's spiel and just sat there, not knowing what to do. Wes filled the air.

"Cat got your tongue, Hank? Look, this is probably very hard to hear and maybe your emotions are running wild and your sphincter is tightening. Look Hank, I kind of need to get security and have them escort you off the premises. It will look like you are taking a leave of absence, we'll say you left to take care of family or maybe you're gonna go write a book for a year. We'll think of something, don't worry about that part. Your job is to shut your face, don't speak to the press. And maybe, maybe, if you lay low long enough, we'll let you back in a couple of years. Great? Great! OK, you can go, Hank," Wes said.

Hank got up calmly and walked out of Wes's office like a zombie. He took his place between two guards, and followed them to a livery cab waiting to take him to his home. Goodbye, network news job. Hello infamy, shame and disgrace. It was going to be a long ride home. Hank fell into the backseat silently, leaned to one side, and cried all the way.

Chapter 3

Hank was freaking out. His job was over. The sharks were in the water, swimming around his fame, and they smelled his blood. His usually ultra-cool demeanor had worked loose and it showed in his face as he arrived on the palatial grounds of his real home, the family house in Connecticut. His place in New York was for when he worked work late or lied about working late to have affairs. This home was where his wife and lovely children lived.

"Honey, I'm home! Where are my beautiful wife and brilliant children?" Hank called.

He walked around the house calling out to them, but found no sign of them. He didn't suspect anything was wrong until he got to the bedroom and found an interesting display on the console table.

There was a bottle of bourbon, a small piece of paper and a tidy stack of legal documents with a fancy felt pen on the top.

He gulped. No, it couldn't be, he thought. Hank had always believed that sooner or later his philandering and general asshole behavior would wreck his marriage. He just thought he could get away with it until the children went off to college. But as he read the note it became clear to him that he had severely underestimated his wife's intellect and cunning.

It read:
Dear Hank,
You asshole. You square-

*jawed, fart-faced asshole. If you
are reading this that means that I
have left you. I have taken the
children and any sentimental
belongings and left you all the
other stupid shit you bought from
SkyMall.*

*You may be wondering why I
left. If you are so stupid you didn't
see the signs, then I'm not sorry,
because you brought this on
yourself, you lying, cheating
bastard.*

*So let me spell this out. I have
left you because:*

*1. I found out you were
grinding up birth control pills and
putting them in the coffee... that
you made for the babysitter!*

*2. I found that bag of white
power you were hiding... under*

our daughter's mattress.

3. I found that gun you were hiding... also under our daughter's mattress.

4. I found that little black book that you thought I'd never find and was surprised to find an entry for my old boss. She had 4 stars next to her name and number.

5. Your pharmacy called the home phone by accident and left a message that your prescription of herpes medication still hadn't been picked up, and it was for your 4th refill.

6. I saw your Internet browser history and managed to guess your password to one of the three bookmarked escort message boards you seem to frequent. And I read some of your wonderfully *helpful reviews of Goldiethong347, posted during the week we were celebrating our 15th wedding anniversary in Santa Barbara. I guess you did not go golfing with an old school chum that day, you asshole.*

7. Lucky number seven. I get a call from some guy who tells me to look at this link. I go to the website, and see you've been lying about what happened in Iraq. The guy who called was actually there. He called the house to set the record straight after he saw the website. His name is Darryl, and boy, am I glad he called. He told me that your assignment ended one week before you said it did. And he also set the record straight on your nightly activities in the Green Zone! Give my best to Private First Class Angela "Easy Pickens" Tennelli. Darryl said she had a kid about 9 months after you left.

So goodbye, you have made a schmuck out of me for the last time. I hope you get Ebola and die, pig!

Love,

Peggy Malone, formerly known as Peggy Pendleton

P.S. If you don't sign those divorce papers in the next 48 hours, you will never see that black book of lovers' names again. But the wonderful Internet will. Every single scanned page! Serves you right for never going digital, you piece of shit!

Hank, having been defeated once already on this day, was defeated again. He sat mildly on his bed, popped some anti-anxiety medication, a handful of sleeping pills, a few hits of Jamaican Gold, and fell back. The bed that had given him so much pleasure now felt like a coffin. He wondered if he had taken too many sleeping pills. He didn't care. He was going to roll the dice on that one.

"God, if you are listening… kill me now. Please!" he prayed as his eyelids lowered and he drifted off to sleep.

Chapter 4

When she packed up her things, left her "Dear Hank" letter and put the kids firmly with her mother, she only had one thing to do next. She would phone Dr. Romo on the booty-call line and hope he answered.

Dr. Romo Esteban had met Peggy Pendleton at a routine teeth cleaning at his dental practice. He was walking to his office when he saw her, head bent back, mouth gaping wide. She had spritz and crap flying out of her mouth as the dental hygienist worked the tools of the trade. He peeked into the treatment room and fell in love.

Too bad for him, she was married then, but he'd held onto the hope that someday she'd leave that newsman of hers. Now the day had arrived. And as it turns out, Peggy Pendleton wanted Dr. Romo to drop his pants as fast as she wanted to drop the Pendleton name.

"The dentist will be with you shortly," the petite, young, very perky nurse says as she closes the door behind Peggy.

"Peggy." His voice is husky, tinged with that sexy accent of his.

She nods at him and stretches out her hand.

"Romo."

He takes two steps toward her, ignoring her outstretched hand and wrapping his strong arms around her waist, pulling her in.

"*Take your pants off,*" she commands.

"*Take off your blouse, Peggy,*' Romo commands back.

They both comply. Romo starts at her breasts. He eases one cup of her bra down and caresses his thumb across her aching nipple. Her stomach tightens with each bit of pressure. Her legs fall open and her pink folds open too, already wet with her nectar. She is shaking.

He leans forward, his hand caressing from her breast down her ribs and then over her stomach. His fingers trace the pink petals of her sex. He nuzzles his nose close under her clit and breathes in.
She screams. She grinds her

pussy onto his face. Romo eases a finger into her. He adds a second finger, then a third, stretching her, preparing her. She bucks and the action drives his digits deep into her sheath. He pumps briskly a few times, hearing the slap of her wet folds as he pummels her wet snatch.

Standing up, he gathers her wrists in his hand and lifts them over her head. He steps between her thighs, forces them apart, and without wasting a single second, drives his cock into her pussy. She screams a second time.

Releasing her wrists, he grabs her upper thighs and lifts her legs off the chair. He hauls her pelvis flush to his groin and rams her into oblivion. She writhes, shudders, and shrieks as wave after wave of orgasm takes her by surprise. It has been years since she's come so much. Her folds are swollen and still she urges him on with whispered pleas.

He finishes with a flourish. Cock glistening with her moisture, he pulls out as he erupts, bathing her stomach with his come.

Peggy baked in the afterglow of the sex and the red heat of the dentist's chair light.

"Isn't this great? That bastard is getting what's coming to him. And I'm about to get mine!" she said smugly.

Meanwhile, in the tony office housing the network newsroom floor, Clint Pascalle was finishing up his makeup. He was the back-up for Hank and anchored the nightly news on the weekends.

This had been his task for seven years. Seven really fucking long years, in Clint's mind. He was far more educated than Hank, and just as experienced. Yet he couldn't connect with the folks as well. So as long as Hank was in the picture, Clint would always be second banana.

But now Hank was out. And Clint became the first banana, second banana, third banana and the only hope for the network's banana. He was working hard to fill the job and bring back some credibility and stability to the failing network news division.

It was his first day as interim anchor, and it felt great to be wearing the big boy shoes for once. But before he could make his big close up happen, he had to meet his new intern, Ms. Jessie

Diamond. She was helping him get acquainted with his new office. She had to show him all the secrets and benefits that office held.

He was at his new desk, marveling at how modern chic it was. There were so many little drawers and compartments. Jessie spent a lot of time showing him where Hank stashed everything. She was wearing a V-neck sweater with no bra, and each time she bent down to open a lower drawer he got a peek at the secrets of her spinner body. She surely knew he was taking some quick peeks. She sure was cool with it. With Hank out of the picture, it was time to make nice with the new king of news nights.

Clint offered some sage advice.

"You know, if it hurts your back to keep bending over like that, why don't you just sit on my lap and tell me about this lovely art on the wall."

"You wouldn't mind? Really?" Jessie said.

"Mind? Jessie Diamond, that would be just fine," Clint whispered in her ear.

She obliged and sat her fanny on his pleated wool pants, sensing that the "semi" underneath would be growing up to be a full "chub-on" any minute now. As she leaned in and pointed to the Rosenquist behind him, her ample breasts squeezed against his chest. How could a hard nipple be felt through a wool sweater, suit, shirt and a tie? Who knew? Who cared? Clint just sat and enjoyed it.

"Isn't this great? That Hank is getting what's coming to him. And I'm about to get mine!" Clint said out loud. And silently he thought, "Aaaah, it's good to be the king!"

Meanwhile, in the hip, urban and millennial office of Fuzzbeed, CEO Nick Luthor was reading the latest click and page view statistics. His website traffic was going through the roof. Venture capital firms were ringing his phone off the hook trying to pump more funding into his media firm. And his firm boner was being pumped by the VP reaching around his waist.

Nick was the king of his own little media mini-empire. His Vice President of Information Technology was an old college buddy who had been with him since the beginning. They were fuck buddies back at Harvard, and they were fuck buddies at the Fuzzbeed offices now.

"You'd think that stupid bastard would have learned. He just kept lying and fucking up. Sooner or later, a man gets caught with the pants down. Right?" Nick said.

"Oh, Nick, you're so bad. You need to be spanked!" VP Rie Honda said.

She enjoyed spanking Nick as much as he loved receiving slaps on his fanny. He had spared no expense installing sound-proof walls to muffle the punishment that Rie inflicted on her bossy boss daily. Rie preferred a leather riding crop on bare skin. She push pushed him face down on his desk.

He was bigger than her, but he bended to her will. She smacked him over and over again as he smiled wide while looking at his phone. He and was reading all the good news around the net about the demise of Hank Pendleton.

"Yup, money's rolling in, clicks are up. Isn't this great? Ow! That Hank, ow, is getting what's coming to him. And I'm about to get mine! Ow!!!"

Meanwhile, Hank's producer, Barry Dreck was packing his office shit into a salty-looking cardboard box. He was not the king of anything. He was the captain of Hank's shipwreck. And when all the underlings and writers on his team scrammed to greener pastures in new departments, it was Barry who was left holding the bag of stink that Hank had opened.

Barry knew that there were people just loving the fact that old Hank was going down. They were going to get theirs. All Barry had to show for it was a gambling vig he couldn't pay, a sore on his balls the doctors couldn't identify, and a huge stain on his resume that would put any news organization on high alert. He just wanted to get out of there. Maybe he could beat the rush hour traffic to the Verrazano Bridge, where he could walk to the edge and jump. That's how bad he felt.

It turned out that the traffic wasn't too bad. He could commit suicide much sooner! He parked the car to the side and put his blinkers on. He exited the vehicle, climbed over the barricade and stepped onto a tiny ledge overlooking the Lower Bay waters. He gulped, tightened his stomach and found the courage in him to end his misery. He had no job, no future, no wife, no children and no hope. No one would miss ol' Barry.

"Time to get mine. I brought this on myself!" he muttered.

He bowed his legs and was getting ready to jump when his cellphone rang.

"Hello? What?!? Really?!? I'll be there in 30 minutes, shit, make that 40 minutes!" Barry exclaimed.

Chapter 5

The haze of chemical-assisted slumber was something Hank Pendleton knew well. Before a deadly dose of medicine kills a man, it lulls him into some deep REM sleep. Hank was in the throes of a very powerful and realistic dream where he was living a totally different reality.

There he was, a few pounds lighter, hair a little blacker and his dick a little chubbier. He was bathing in a hot tub with his hero of all heroes, the great communicator, Ofra Wimpry. And she was commending him on his great work. She also kept going on and on about how great it was that he was helping urban youth.

"Well, you know, Ofra, I can't prove it, but dang it, I always knew there was a little black in me. Ya dig?" Hank cooed towards the foxy lady.

Then, without asking, she put her arms around him. Her face was very close to his and there was yearning in her eyes. He was trying to move into a wet kiss when all of a sudden he felt very wet all over, and not in the good way.

"Ah!!! I'm drowning!" he yelled. *SLAP! SLAP! SLAP!*

"No sir, you are not drowning. You are still in your bed. Please relax and sit up!" said a voice from above.

Hanks rubbed his awoken eyes and then saw a stocky yet fit gentleman he had never seen before.

"Who the hell are you? And why are you in my house?" he asked.

"No time to talk, drink this."

The man shoved a shot full of gray goo into Hank's mouth and firmly held his jaw closed, forcing him to drink it. Hank squirmed and writhed and tried to get free, but the man was too strong. Then some other men surrounded him and held his face down over a bucket. *BLORCH!*

All of his partially digested medication, booze and lunch exploded out of his mouth. He gasped and barfed in the bucket and on his floor. It was awful and painful, and most of it all, it was confusing. Who were these men? What were they doing here?

The stocky man backed up, took a seat on the corner chaise lounge and threw off the gloves and rags protecting him from the projectile vomit.

"Sir, my name is Agent Arthur Bennett, and I'm with the Department of Homeland Security. We tried ringing your bell, but got no answer, so we kicked the door down and walked in. And you're welcome, we just saved your life."

"You can't do that! You can't just barge into my house!" Hank protested.

"We're the federal government, and you are high on some pretty illegal shit, so shut up and let me do the talking. And wipe your face, goddamnit! Anyway, we would like to ask you some questions about that trip to Iraq you reported about."

"Whoa! I can explain! Please."

"Shut up! I'm not going to say it one more time! You went to Iraq and were in the trio of choppers that went down, just like in your story, right?" Beckett asked.

"Um, you said shut up, can I answer?" Hank said.

"Yes!"

"Then yes. I was there. That is the honest to God truth."

"Good, do you know this man?"

Beckett held up a big letter-size picture of an Army Private. It was the same man who had called Hank's wife.

"Yeah! That asshole called my wife about it. He started this whole mess. Cost me my job!"

"Well, that asshole, Darryl Mixon, was running a scam with another soldier named Lori Lee. They were the ones who gave you the drugs in Iraq, and they were the ones who showed you around those special massage parlors where they don't ask questions. Yes. Them! Well, at the end of the war, they went AWOL. They got into some heavy shit, and recently these fuckers have been selling weapons to ISIS."

"What? Who's Isis? That dog on Downton Abbey?" Hank asked confusedly.

"Are you fucking kidding

me? You did a report on ISIS last week!"

"I only read the news, I don't ingest it. Ow, my head hurts."

Agent Beckett rolled his eyes. Hank Pendleton was clearly a moron. But then, in slow, grade-school level speech, Beckett outlined the broad strokes of a major case his squad had been investigating. And because of Hank's screw-up, they'd gotten a big break in the case.

"We've been looking for these two for years. Couldn't find them. But now that you pissed him off with that news story, he's resurfaced. We know he called your wife, and the call came from a phone right here in New York. Seems he has surfaced and wants to make a buck off of your scandal."

"How?" Hank asked.

"They have a really bad video of you doing really bad things. I'm sure you know what I'm talking about. They've held on to it for years, and now that your downfall is a page-one story around the world, they are going to cash in their chips big time. They already contacted a bunch of sleazy websites, including Fuzzbeed. The going rate is a cool million."

"Shit. Well, what do you want from me?" Hank asked.

"We want to use you to get to them. We want you to reach out to them and make them an even higher offer. You're the only one with a motive big enough to make that sum believable. And you are the only one they would trust to truly pay top dollar to keep this quiet. And we want you to set up a meeting, where you hand them over a suitcase of cash, and we swoop in and grab them."

"Like a sting operation?!?" Hank squealed.

"Yes, you blathering moron, a sting operation!"

"I'll do it. If we pull this off I'll be a hero! A fucking hero. Every network will want me!" Hank enthused.

"You don't have a choice. Now clean yourself up. Here are details."

Agent Beckett handed over a hefty brown file folder with all the information on the case. It outlined how to contact the pair, how to offer them money and where to set up the meeting. It was real cloak-and-dagger type spy shit, and Hank was loving it.

He looked up and for a second got lost in his own imagination. He saw his old anchor chair. He saw his old life. It was in his grasp! He knew that if there was something America loved more than tearing down a celebrity, it was a glorious comeback!

"OK. Let's do this!" he exclaimed.

Agent Beckett finally smiled a toothy grin. There was nothing he loved more than catching a bad guy.

"But first, call your producer.

That Barry guy. We're gonna need him too," Beckett said.

Chapter 6

Barry never told Hank he was about to jump off a bridge. He only took the call and agreed to meet him. Since he was a child, Barry had loved James Bond movies. And as soon as he was asked to take part in a sting operation, his life seemed to have meaning again. He quickly got in his car and met Hank at the meeting place.

Hank usually wore suits, and of course looked like an anchor. For the operation, he had to look like a wanker. He had a ruffled military jacket and a seaman's hat tucked down over his eyes. He looked ridiculous. It never occurred to Barry why he was asked to be there. It was all for show. His job was just to stand there by Hank. Prideful men always kept flunkies with them. And for this meeting, that flunky was Barry. The two men waited by the side of Hank's Audi TT in the empty parking lot next to the abandoned factory near the old pier. And in the floors of the factory, hiding in the shadows, were Agent Beckett and a number of armed officers waiting in the wings.

When the clock struck 11, the game was on. A nondescript white van approached. Hank could feel the hairs on the back of his neck stick up with excitement. Barry's balls tingled with fearfulness. Neither one had any regrets about being in this position, but they sure didn't want to die either. They were dealing with trained killers, and they both knew that.

The vehicle stopped, and two

shady looking motherfuckers got out. One man, one woman. The man was Darryl Mixon and he looked like someone had dipped him in dirt-colored dye, dragged him through a bramble bush and tattooed over any clean spots left. He was really scary looking, and much bigger than Hank remembered. He also wore an army jacket and his had a 9mm peeking out from a holster inside.

The woman who got out was Lori Lee. Lori looked much better, but only because she was younger than Darryl and seemed like she showered regularly. The petite pale brunette stayed 10 paces behind Darryl as they approached the newbie news-spies.

"How's it hanging, Hank? You look well. So we gonna do dis or what?" Darryl said with much spittle.

Darryl stood menacingly while Lorie just stood behind him, running her fingers over the handle of her large knife. Her eyes burned through Barry as she successfully tried to intimidate him further. Hank decided to "man up" and take charge of the conversation.

"Hey, Darryl. You have something I want. And I have something you want," Hank said with a confidence that masked how scared he was. He stood tall and proud and turned out to be a better actor than Agent Beckett had thought.

Back in the surveillance van, parked inside the warehouse, Agent Beckett watched the action intently. He had several agents with very big guns at the ready.

They huddled around a small monitor to watch the action filmed by secret little cameras placed around the complex.

"He's good. This may actually work," Beckett said.

Darryl pulled out a small canister with a miniDV tape inside.

"Yeah, I got what you want, Hank. High-def video of you whoring young pretty things. You betting at the child camel races with 'questionable' crime families. You buying that gorilla skin hat from the secret room at the bazaar. So I know you wouldn't want this to fall into the hands of Fuzzbeed, or any other set of hands. Cause they're asking! And you better pay better than them!"

"Darryl, all I can say is, you got me! Red-handed. Now, I have this case of money to trade for that tape. What you say we make a switcheroo and go our merry ways?" Hank said.

They stared each other down like two buckaroos in a Sergio Leone film, and when the music in their heads paused they approached each other's space. With outstretched hands they presented their merchandise and gifted the prizes to each other, then took careful steps back.

Hank had done it! Now he just had to watch the two evildoers drive away and allow them to get caught by the squad car waiting in the alley that led out to the highway.

"Well, Darryl, thanks for the

business."

"Yeah, you stay frosty Hank, see you around," Darryl said.

Barry, who hadn't said shit the whole time, started to feel his stiffy coming back as he realized that they'd just pulled it off. Hank got one too, and used the tape canister to hide it. They were almost home free. Yet, right then, Hank's stupidity had to screw it all up.

Hank put his finger to his ear to press on the hidden earpiece that connected him to the surveillance van. It was a dumb rookie move that Lori happened to catch.

She grabbed Darryl's arm and stopped him from getting back in the van.

"Hey! Hey, asshole, turn around!" Lori ordered.

Hank's heart dropped and Barry cried when they realized that they'd fucked up. They both turned around slowly and put on their best poker faces.

"You wearing a wire, Pendleton?!? You setting us up?!?" Lori demanded.

She fumed and turned beet red. She pulled out her knife and pointed it their way. She meant business. And the only thing worse than her was her cranked up boyfriend, who had pulled out his 9mm and pointed it their way too. Hank and Barry were terrified.

"You know what, Hank? I think I'm gonna take that tape

back. It'll be worth just as much when you're dead!"

Darryl raised his gun and aimed it at Hank's head. This was it, Hank thought. His number was up and he would die as a disgrace. He closed his eyes and expected the blackness to become permanent when he heard a bullhorn in the distance. Agent Beckett had decided to make a move and announced it via the loudspeaker on top of the surveillance van. It was a feeble effort to save Hank and Barry's lives.

"Darryl Mixon and Lori Lee. We have you surrounded. Put your weapons down and place your hands on top of your heads," Beckett yelled out.

Darryl spun around and

started to point his gun in all directions, looking for the source of the bullhorn's noise. He fired a few errant rounds into the distance just to make a point. Squad cars started to file in from the alley. He fired at them, killing the driver of the lead car. Then the car spun to the side and blocked the passage of the other squad cars. The officers returned fire but missed.

With bullets leaving guns so rapidly, Hank ran for it, but in the dumbest way possible. As he turned, he tripped over his own foot! He fell down but didn't have time to protect his head, and it hit the side of a piece of scrap wood on the ground. The blow knocked him out and made him an easy target. Barry, seeing his only friend in mortal danger, grabbed Hank's ankles and started pulling him to the side and out of harm's way.

Barry was a full five inches shorter than Hank, and hauling his ass was no easy feat. But he was able to make it to the edge of the open parking clearing and shove Hank under a tipped forklift. Then he turned around to see if he could help the officers. It was all quite brave, and his actions even surprised Barry himself. It was as if another man was calling the shots in his brain and his meager pussy-fart self was nowhere to be found.

He had started running in the direction of a fallen officer who'd been hit when he was tackled from the side by the vicious beauty, Lori Lee. Darryl's gunfire was still blasting everywhere when she plowed into Barry's side with her shoulder. The impact cracked several ribs and knocked him to the ground. Then she picked up a loose pipe and started bashing his legs in. She broke his bones so he couldn't run away.

"Ah!!!" Barry called out. He was in terrible pain, and all his efforts to fight off Lori seemed to be failing. She was fast, and for each punch or swat he tried to make, she met him and slashed at his arms with her massive knife. Then she pinned him down, one leg over each side of him.

"Please don't kill me!" Barry begged.

"OK. Sure. With that great begging job, I guess I'll have to let you go," Lori deadpanned.

Barry's eyes widened. He was ecstatic thinking that it might work!

"Thank you! You're…" Barry was cut off by the swing of the big knife slicing his gullet wide open. The only sound he made was *gurgle-gurgle* as blood flowed freely from his neck. Some blood spurted up and onto Lori, and some blood oozed out slowly and surrounded his body like a growing red shadow on the ground.

Lori smiled at her handiwork. She couldn't help but admire how cleanly she'd cut, and how deeply. He was dying so fast that a small wiggle of his fingers was his only sign of life. And soon his little pinky stopped moving, although she could still see the terrified expression on his face. She felt nothing for the good man she had just murdered. She had killed so many men before. And planned on killing many more in her lifetime.

As gunplay continued between Darryl and the outnumbering group of lawmen, the bullets curiously ignored Lori even though she was only 50 feet away from the action. She had time to turn slowly and clean her knife while she sought her next prey. It was the passed-out body of that snitch Hank that her knife's edge yearned for. She would be glad to serve it up shortly.

She walked over and stood over above Hank with her blade pointing downwards. It was pointing at his head. It looked like she was going to be kind to Hank and kill him instantly with a stab to the brain. In his slumber, he would feel nothing.

"This is more than you

deserve, you pig," she said coldly, and spat at his face.

Then she lifted her knife and held it there for a split second. As it was raised over her head, that split second of pause was all it took for Agent Beckett to fire an armor-piercing bullet through the elbow of Lori's right arm. It hit the bone and shattered upon impact, taking chunks of skin and cartilage with it. Lori's arm was blown almost clean off; only the thinnest flap of skin remained to hold her forearm and her bicep together.

Lori cried out, and that certainly got everyone's attention. The firefight between Darryl and the officers stopped for a collective moment. Then the battle resumed. Lori fell down, grabbed her sidearm and returned fire at Agent Beckett. As she used her gun, blood jetted from her severed veins and turned her pant leg completely red.

Agent Beckett continued to volley shots as Lori took cover behind a steel girder column nearby. They both were missing their targets now.

"Give it up! You'll bleed out in a minute. We can get you to a hospital!" Agent Beckett pleaded. Lori certainly was in bad shape, but everything about her looked like she was not going to give up. If she was going to die, she was taking some more people with her. Figuring that Agent Beckett was the harder target, she turned around and re-focused on the passed out anchorman.

Hank was facedown, lifeless, sleeping through all of the

mayhem. Lori popped up, cradling her bad arm, and started running towards him. She had only about 10 feet to go. Beckett saw this and chased after her, firing as he ran. He was aiming for her head and back, but kept missing. He grazed her leg, but barely. It didn't stop her, and she was getting ever closer to poor Hank.

Agent Beckett decided to stop, kneel and aim properly. Maybe then he'd be able put her down. He drew a bead on Lori Lee's head. He had her in his sights. She reached Hank and swung her weapon forward. One of them was going to strike first.

Bam! Lori's frontal lobe and bits of skull and blood exploded from the front of her head and landed on Hank's sleeping face. And the rest of her lifeless body fell around like him like a corpse Snuggie. He had no idea how close he was to death.

Agent Beckett stumbled forward, puffed with pride at how good a shot he was. "One terrorist down, one to go,", he thought. But while he was playing sharpshooter, Darryl was shooting fish in a barrel. He had picked off three officers, and still they had not hit him. His special forces training showed. And now he needed to escape.

Darryl jumped into his car, and keeping his head down, plowed forward. He ran over Barry's body and started speeding toward the pier. He figured he could take his chances in the water, since crashed vehicles blocked the only exit. It was a desperate measure for a desperate man.

But then he glimpsed something that chilled him to the bone. It was his partner in crime and partner in life, Lori Lee, dead as a side of beef on the ground.

"You bastards!" he screamed.

He fumed and hit the gas pedal, hoping to avenge her death, for straight ahead in his path was a hobbling Agent Beckett. The chassis of Darryl's ride accelerated toward Beckett like a battering ram. And Beckett could not jump out of the way in time. So he jumped up and landed right on the hood of Darryl's car.

He was hit at close to 30 miles an hour, but he didn't fly off the hood once he hit it. No, he clung to it, losing his gun in the process. He looked back and saw that Darryl, in his rage, intended to drive right off the pier at full speed. They would probably both die, but Darryl didn't care anymore. He was going out in a blaze of glory, or rather a splash of revenge.

The good guy and the bad guy looked into each other's eyes for one last second. It was contempt all around, but no sadness. They both knew the dangers of the lives they led. As the car sped off of the pier, they only mouthed the words "fuck you" through the windshield glass as the car flew through the air into the icy cold bay.

It splashed in and the impact against the water killed Agent Beckett instantly. Darryl saw the dead agent float off as he sank deeper into the water. The rising water pressure kept him from opening the car doors, and soon water poured in. Having lost Lori, he gave up trying and let the dirty water fill his lungs. It was a painful and disgusting way to go.

On the ground, surrounded by wounded cops, were a dead terrorist and a dead best friend. Hank was still passed out, no doubt dreaming of something pleasant, dirty and wrong.

Chapter 7

A season had passed since the firefight in New York. It was a snowy evening all over Manhattan. Despite the tough weather, hundreds of the finest in journalism, media and entertainment were braving the cold to see something amazing.

Tonight was the night that Hank Pendleton was going to accept the Empire State Award from the governor of New York for his courageous efforts in thwarting an international smuggling and terrorism operation. It was to be the first time that Hank Pendleton had made a public appearance since his fall from grace and return to superstardom.

In all of the news reports on the sting operation, Hank was

indeed lauded as a hero. And in the minds of the average TV viewer and network executive, he was forgiven for his tiny white lies about the war. People felt that he had suffered enough and certainly redeemed himself by his brave actions.

The story of what really happened that night varied from source to source. Hank's network was going to broadcast these awards as his big comeback, with the stipulation that he tell the real story of what happened for the first time. That would garner lots of attention and ratings.

The crowd was full of people who had profited off of Hank's initial demise, but were now showing a different face as they hoped to be associated with him once more.

There was Peggy Pendleton, now going by her ex-husband's name again. Next to her was Dr. Romo Esteban, showing his pearly whites and holding his lovely new girlfriend. There was the CEO of Fuzzbeed, Nick Luthor, with his new girlfriend of the month. Clint Pascalle was there too, with a fake smile on his face and daggers shooting from his eyes. And there in the very front were the widow and family of Agent Beckett, who were holding a framed picture of him.

The lights went down and out came the governor. He was a portly blue-collar bear of a man who spoke with a Bronx cheer drawl.

"You know, we throw around the word 'hero' all the time. But it's rare that it really fits the man we're using it on. Tonight, I am pleased to present a man who does fit that description. A man who, like all of us New Yorkers, didn't quit when the chips were down. He fought back and found redemption and put some bad guys in the ground while he was at it. Ladies and gentlemen, please put your hands together for Mr. Hank Pendleton!"

"Hooray!" "Huzzah!" "Yeea booyeee!"

Crazy, thunderous applause poured out of every crevice in the auditorium as a rested, healed and dapper Hank Pendleton took the stage. He waved his hands for a full minute, soaking in the affection and adoration he'd thought he would never feel again. And as always, Hank was a consummate professional as he shed a tear and waved at the family of Agent Beckett before giving a proud thumbs-up to his own family and the whole of America that was watching.

"Good evening. It's great to be back," he said.

More applause filled the theater. It was going to be that kind of a night for him.

"Please, please. Thank you. Thank you. Friends, I just want to say that I am the luckiest man on the face of the earth. I stood on the edge and looked into the dark abyss and there, waiting for me, were the cold eyes of Death. I thought I would fall in, but no, I was pulled out and brought back to the light by a great man. I thank Agent Beckett for that."

The crowd clapped and honored the family of Agent Beckett for a few seconds before quieting again and waiting to hear more of Hank's speech. But Hank paused. He looked down at his notes, and saw a glowing dedication to Agent Beckett's bravery and sacrifice. The news had reported different accounts of what really happened. Through the smoke and haze of gunpowder, many officers swore they'd seen different things. Some even said that Hank didn't pass out until the end. Hank's speech, which was pieced together from what he'd seen on the news, made Agent Beckett the hero. Hank was, of course, passed out and had no memory of what happened.

He looked out into the crowd. There were so many beautiful

faces there. So much deep and juicy cleavage. The smell of wealth and fancy perfume mixed together into an intoxicating brew around Hank's sensibilities. His balls started to tickle. He started to get that old feeling again. Out in the middle of the crowd, there were at least four A-list actresses staring up at him with their mouths wide open, just waiting for his heroism to rise. This was his night! Not Agent Beckett's night, he thought.

The written version of his speech would place him back in his old chair at the network. The version in his head would place him at the back of at least two of those A-lister's behinds, three if he was lucky. The written version would get him an invite to the best parties on the Upper East Side. The magic version in his head would get him invited to Cannes, Abu Dhabi and the master deck of the Aga Khan's yacht. His balls still tickled, and that old Hank sensibility was bubbling inside of him. He continued.

"I, uh, uh, yes, I thank Agent Beckett for that. I thank him for training me and giving me the skills I needed to take out those evil-doers and stop their reign of terror once and for all. It all started years ago, when I suspected that Darryl Mixon and Lori Lee were up to no good. But they were just suspicions that I couldn't prove. So I waited, and watched, and for years we investigated. Barry, my late producer, and I were thrilled when we found out that they were back in New York. We were eager to help the authorities and do our patriotic chore. We set up the sting in the parking lot. And once we made the switch of goods I pointed at Darryl and said, ''Stop right there, Buster, the jig is up!' Knowing that they wouldn't go quietly, Barry and I lunged before they could get their guns out. I kicked Darryl four feet away with a roundhouse to the chest. Then we double-teamed Lori Lee – who was a twelfth-level black belt in karate and jiu-jitsu, by the way – with our own brand of New York City street-brawler technique. But alas, Barry slipped and his Dragon-Fist uppercut missed its mark, giving Lori a chance to stab him with a shiv she hid in her bra. I tell you, she had a whole arsenal in that bra. I tried to save him, but she just kept coming, so I pulled out the big guns, and by big guns I mean my Mantis-Elbow and the lethal three-point palm Tiger-Strike. Using those and my Cobra-Thrust and

Panda-Stomp, I got her in a Spider-Lock and did an Around the World, disabling her Crab-Claw pincer grip. Knowing she was outmatched, she ran. Then Agent Beckett threw me his peacemaker and I took off in pursuit. Now, I would never shoot an unarmed woman, but let me tell you, she was armed. She pulled out that .38 Special from her panty waist, and in self-defense, I aimed my weapon. I only had a second to process it, a split second, but I remember my marksman training under master six-shooter and shaman "Buffalo" Bob Brickell. He said to me, 'Hank, let the Spirit Eagle guide your eyes, let the Spirit Wolf guide your hand, let the Spirit Scorpion guide your bullet.' I pulled the trigger, and ended her days with a heavy heart. Then I turned to help the officers who were pinned down by Darryl

Mixon's gunfire. That's when he got in his car in tried to ram Agent Beckett and me. We weren't going to let that happen. So, we tried play number B17, the Widow-maker. He gave me a boost, I jumped over the car and he then jumped on its hood. I was to take out the tires, while he took care of the driver, but alas, I was out of bullets. And crazy Darryl Mixon decided to commit suicide instead of flee the scene. I ran after the car and was almost able to grab the back bumper, but a piece flew off, hit me in the head and knocked me out. Damn, we were so close! Some might say that sounds too incredible. But you know, when you are a professional journalist, it's all in a day's work. Am I right?!?"

The crowed jumped to their feet and applauded. The men fist

pumped in excitement. The women jumped and jiggled, trying to get superstar Hank's attention. One camera even caught a stray pair of panties fly up on the stage with a Twitter handle written in lipstick. It was good to be Hank Pendleton again.

Hank just beamed at the crowd and gave them what they wanted. Then he spontaneously started doing one-arm push-ups. The crowd went wild. Even Agent Beckett's widow cheered him on. As he pumped his body up and down, Hank had learned nothing. As he looked up and smiled a toothy grin for the camera, he had not changed at all. But Hank didn't care. He never really had and never would. And with his signature line he yelled his heart out.

"Thank you for watching and good night and sleep tight America!!!"

The End